This
MOUSE WORKS
Classics Collection Storybook

belongs to

_____

DISNEY's Aladdin

Adapted by Don Ferguson

MOUSE WORKS

Also available in Spanish

© 1992, 1993, 1996 Disney Enterprises, Inc.
Printed in the United States of America
ISBN: 1-57082-030-9
3 5 7 9 10 8 6 4

Once, in a faraway land, there was a
boy who lived in the streets . . . a
girl who lived in a palace . . . and a
genie who lived in a lamp . . .

It was midnight on the vast Arabian desert. Silhouetted against the moon, a horseman waited. Suddenly, out of the shadows, a second mounted figure appeared, his galloping horse churning up the desert sand.

3

In a moment, the two horsemen met.

"You're late, Gazeem!" growled the first.

"A thousand apologies, Great Jafar!" Gazeem whined. "But see – I have brought the missing half of the scarab medallion!"

"At last!" Jafar hissed, pulling the other half of the medallion from his robe.

"Look, Iago!" Jafar said to the parrot on his shoulder. Jafar joined the two halves. "A perfect fit!"

As the two halves touched, the scarab glowed, and a crack of thunder shattered the desert silence! The scarab sprang from Jafar's hand and sped away over the dunes.

"Follow the trail!" Jafar exclaimed, spurring his horse into action. "It will lead us to the Cave of Wonders!"

The horsemen followed the magic scarab far into the desert. At last it stopped its flight and buried itself in a mound of sand.

Then, in a crash of thunder and lightning, the sand rose up to form a huge tiger's head, between whose open jaws was the entrance to . . .

"The Cave of Wonders!" Jafar exclaimed.

"Do not forget my reward, Great Jafar! I braved great danger to steal the missing half of the medallion for you!"

"The treasure in the cave is your reward, Gazeem!" Jafar replied. "But first, you must bring me the lamp!"

Gazeem rushed eagerly into the darkness of the tiger's mouth. Instantly, the gigantic jaws slammed shut on the thief!

"Unworthy fool!" boomed the voice of the tiger-god. "Only one whose worth is buried deep within a diamond in the rough may enter here!"

In the twinkling of an eye, the tiger-head cave, its treasures, and Gazeem had melted back into the desert.

"Awk! Now we'll never get that stupid lamp!" squawked the parrot.

"Patience, Iago!" Jafar said. "Gazeem was obviously not the diamond in the rough. So now we must find the one who is!"

The next morning, in the bustling marketplace of Agrabah a handsome young thief stared down at a scene of complete confusion. Aladdin (for that was the thief's name) had stolen a loaf of bread and escaped onto a rooftop. As he and his pet monkey, Abu, watched, the Sultan's guards searched for him among the market stalls.

Finally the guards gave up, and Aladdin and Abu sat down to eat their first food in days—stale bread.

But Aladdin realized that there were others worse off than he, and he gave the bread away to a couple of hungry children.

"Cheer up, Abu," he said as he made himself as comfortable as he could. "Someday it'll be better than this. Just you wait!"

Meanwhile, in the Sultan's palace, time was running out for Princess Jasmine.

"But, Jasmine, it's the law!" the Sultan insisted. "You must marry a prince by your next birthday! And it will be your birthday in just three days!"

"I don't love Prince Achmed!" Jasmine replied. "Oh, Father! How can you force me to marry someone I don't love?"

Jasmine rushed tearfully into the palace garden.

"Oh, Rajah!" she said to her pet Bengal tiger waiting by the garden pool. "Whatever shall I do?" She looked up at the high wall surrounding the palace. If she could just climb over that wall, she would be free!

Inside the palace, the Sultan was getting desperate. "Jafar," he groaned to his chief advisor, "I must find a husband for Jasmine! She's refused every prince in the land!"

"I think I can help," Jafar said. "But I will need the Mystique Blue Diamond that you wear!"

"No, Jafar! You know it is forbidden for the Sultan to remove the Mystique Blue Diamond!"

Jafar raised his cobra-headed staff and held it hypnotically before the Sultan's eyes.

"You will give me the Diamond!" Jafar commanded slowly.

"Yes . . . Master . . ." the Sultan answered, deep in a trance.

Clutching the Sultan's ring, Jafar stepped into a secret passage and climbed a long flight of stairs to his tower laboratory.

"Our moment draws near, Iago! With this diamond, I can find . . ."

"Awk! A husband for Jasmine?"

"No, fool! The one who can get us the lamp!"

Once over the palace wall, Jasmine had suddenly found herself alone in a world she had never before experienced—Agrabah's bustling marketplace.

Seeing a hungry child, she plucked an apple from a fruit stand and gave it to him.

"You'd better be able to pay for that, you little street urchin!" bellowed the huge fruit seller.

"P-pay?" Jasmine stammered. "B-but I have no money!"

Suddenly a young man emerged from the crowd and stepped between the towering shopkeeper and the frightened girl.

"Forgive my poor sister, oh merciful one!" the young man pleaded. "She didn't mean to steal! She's a little crazy in the head!"

Then he turned to Jasmine. "Come, sister dear. I'll take you to the doctor now."

"Another of your tricks, Aladdin, son of a jackal!" shouted the shopkeeper.

Aladdin seized Jasmine's hand and pulled her into the crowded marketplace, leading her to a rooftop far above the streets. "We'll be safe here!" he said.

Then he turned to the lovely girl. "Where do you come from?" he asked.

"I ran away from home!" Jasmine replied. "My father is trying to force me to get married!"

"Wow!" said Aladdin. "That's awful!"

Meanwhile, in a tower above the palace, Jafar's secret laboratory crackled with lightning bolts as the evil alchemist brought the all-seeing "sands of time" to life.

"Show me the one who can enter the cave!" Jafar commanded.

The swirling sands of time parted, revealing a young man on a rooftop in Agrabah.

"Have the guards bring him to the palace!" Jafar said to Iago.

The palace guards quickly marched into the city, and swarmed up to Aladdin's hiding place. Before Aladdin could leap to his feet, he was a prisoner.

Jasmine threw back her hood. "Release him at once!" the girl ordered.

"Princess Jasmine!" gasped the surprised palace guards.

"*Princess* Jasmine?" gasped the surprised Aladdin.

"I dare not release him, Princess," said the captain of the guards. "My orders come from Jafar. You will have to take it up with him."

"Believe me, I will!" Jasmine said.

In a dungeon cell in the palace, Aladdin thought about the beautiful girl he had rescued from the shopkeeper.

"A princess! I can't believe it!" he said aloud to Abu, who had followed him into the dungeon and freed him from the chains. "And I thought she was as poor as we are!"

Unnoticed, Jafar, disguised as an old prisoner, had slipped quietly into the cell.

"You don't always have to be poor, Aladdin!" he said. "There is a cave filled with treasure! It can be yours if you will just help me get a worthless lamp!"

Eager to get out of the dungeon, Aladdin agreed.

In the middle of the vast desert, the tiger's head rose up before Aladdin's astonished eyes.

"First, bring me the lamp!" Jafar said eagerly. "Then, the treasure will be yours!"

Carefully Aladdin approached the entrance to the cave.

"Who disturbs my slumber?" the voice of the cave thundered.

"Uh . . . it is I . . . Aladdin!"

"Enter, Aladdin!" the voice replied.

Jafar watched Aladdin and Abu enter the cave and disappear into the darkness.

In the eerie glow of the cave, Aladdin and Abu followed steep steps down, down, down, until they found a huge chamber filled with mounds of golden treasure!

"Just a handful of this would make me richer than the Sultan!" Aladdin exclaimed.

Abu reached for a glittering ruby.

"No, Abu!" Aladdin warned. "We mustn't touch *anything* until we find the lamp!"

Suddenly Aladdin and Abu noticed a richly-embroidered carpet peeking at them from behind a pile of gold coins.

"Well, I'll be!" Aladdin laughed. "A magic carpet! Maybe it knows where we can find the lamp."

The magic carpet showed
Aladdin into a second chamber.
High atop a massive altar, he
saw the lamp.

Aladdin ran up the stone
steps. But as the boy was
reaching for the lamp, Abu, who
could never resist a glittering
jewel, grabbed a gem from the
hands of an idol.

The ground began to tremble.
Then the voice of the cave
spoke.

"Abu has touched the
forbidden treasure! You shall
never again see the light of
day!"

The altar began to crumble beneath Aladdin's feet. He snatched the lamp, ran down the swaying stone steps, and jumped aboard the carpet.

The floor of the cavern was turning to molten lava, and Abu was in danger of dying. Aladdin grabbed Abu's paw and pulled him onto the carpet. As the cave began to collapse behind them, the magic carpet sped Aladdin and Abu toward the entrance, where Jafar waited.

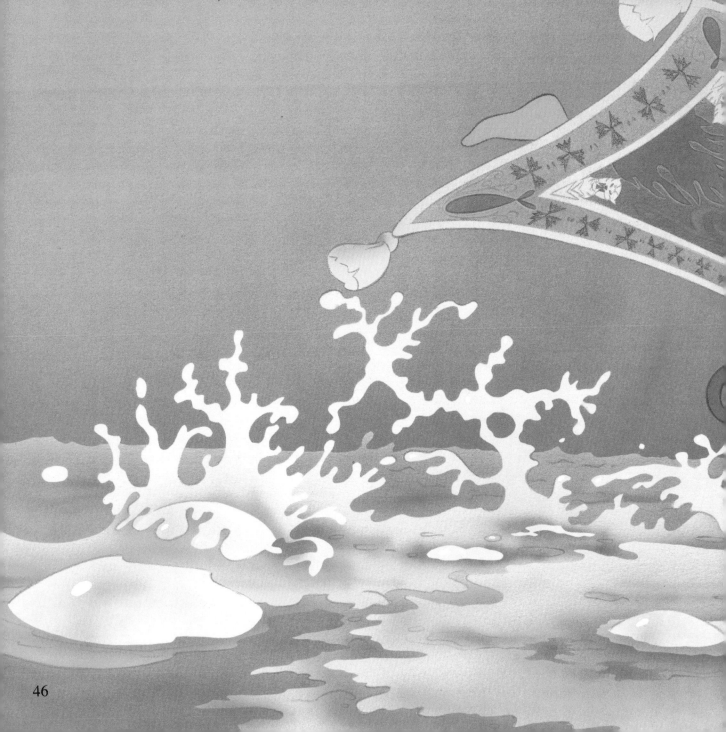

"Old man! Help us!" Aladdin called, clinging to the heaving edge of the cave.

"The lamp! Give me the lamp!" cried Jafar. He seized it from Aladdin's hand!

Then, from his robe, Jafar drew a long, gleaming dagger!

"Good-bye, fool!" Jafar snarled, raising the dagger over the helpless Aladdin!

In a flash, Abu leaped from Aladdin's shoulder.

"Ow!" Jafar shrieked, as the little monkey's teeth bit into his arm. He dropped the dagger. Abu and Aladdin fell back into the cave!

The earthquake had stopped. The cave was as silent as a tomb.

"We're trapped in here, Abu!" Aladdin despaired. "That jackal stole the lamp! Now he'll never come back for us!"

Abu chirped and held up his paw. Aladdin's eyes widened. In Abu's paw was . . .

"The lamp! You got it back when you bit him! Good work, Abu!"

Aladdin took the lamp. "I wonder what's so special about this dusty old thing." He rubbed it, trying to get a better look at it.

The lamp began to glow! Then a towering cloud of smoke poured from the spout! The smoke formed itself into a gigantic figure!

"Say, you're a lot smaller than my last master!" the giant said, looking at Aladdin. "Or maybe I've gotten bigger over the last ten thousand years!"

"Are you the genie of the lamp?" Aladdin asked.

"The one and only!" the genie replied.

"I don't believe you! If you were a real genie, you could get us out of this cave!"

"Oh, yeah?" the genie said to Aladdin. "Well, watch this, Mister Smarty-Pants!"

Quick as a wink they were out of the cave, soaring over the desert on the magic carpet.

"How's that, kiddo? Am I a genie, or am I a genie?"

"I guess you're a genie, all right!" Aladdin said. "So, do I get three wishes?"

"Yep!" said the genie. "But no fair wishing for three more wishes!"

Aladdin thought of the Princess Jasmine.

"I wish . . . I wish to be a prince!"

When Jafar returned to the palace, he came face to face with a very angry princess.

"I command you to release Aladdin!"

"But, Princess, Aladdin has already been executed!" Jafar lied.

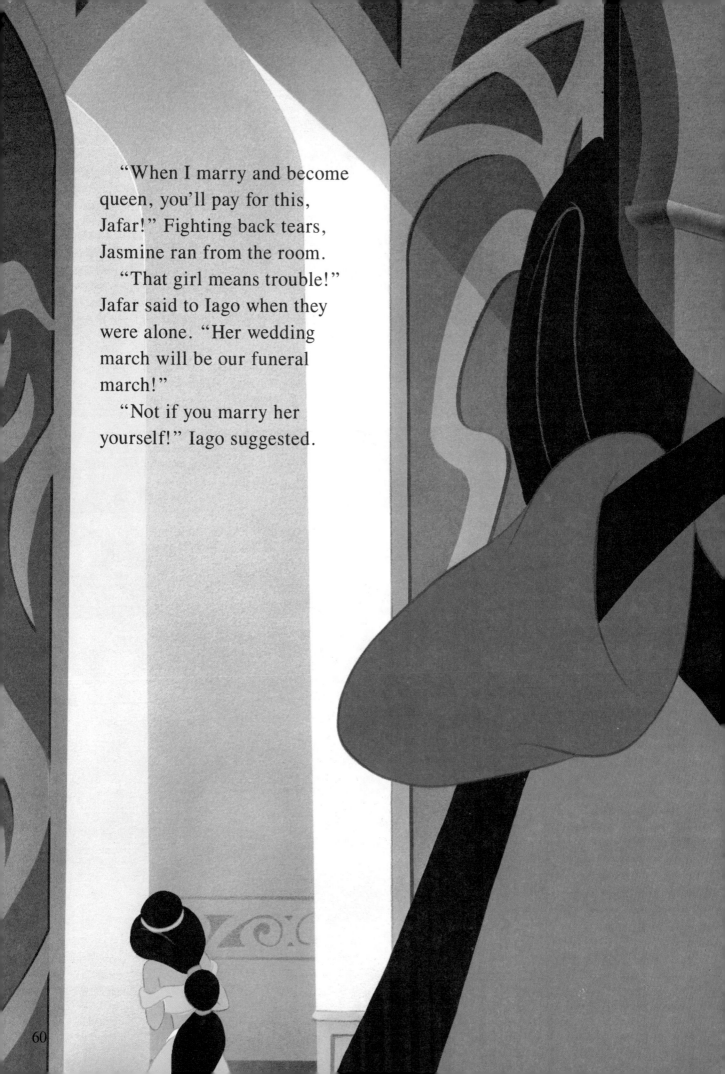

"When I marry and become queen, you'll pay for this, Jafar!" Fighting back tears, Jasmine ran from the room.

"That girl means trouble!" Jafar said to Iago when they were alone. "Her wedding march will be our funeral march!"

"Not if you marry her yourself!" Iago suggested.

Suddenly, the palace gates
were thrown open.

"Prince Ali of Ababwa!"
announced a palace guard.
Trumpets blared! Drums rolled!
And into the palace flew
Aladdin on his magic carpet!

He was dressed from turban
to toe in the silks and jewels of a
royal prince!

"I have come to seek the hand
of the Princess Jasmine," he said
to the astonished Sultan.

That night when Prince Ali took Jasmine for a moonlight ride on his magic carpet, she discovered that he was the same young man she had met in the marketplace.

Far below, Jafar watched them, "I must get rid of that intruder before he spoils my plans!" he thought.

By the time the carpet had returned to the palace, Jasmine knew the man she wanted to marry.

"Goodnight, my prince . . . Aladdin!" she said, going into her bedchamber.

At once, Jafar and his guards fell upon Aladdin!

Bound and gagged, Aladdin was carried to the edge of a high cliff. Below, he could hear angry waves crashing.

"So you like to fly, Prince Ali?" Jafar said. "Well, try this!" The guards threw Aladdin over the cliff, into the waiting sea!

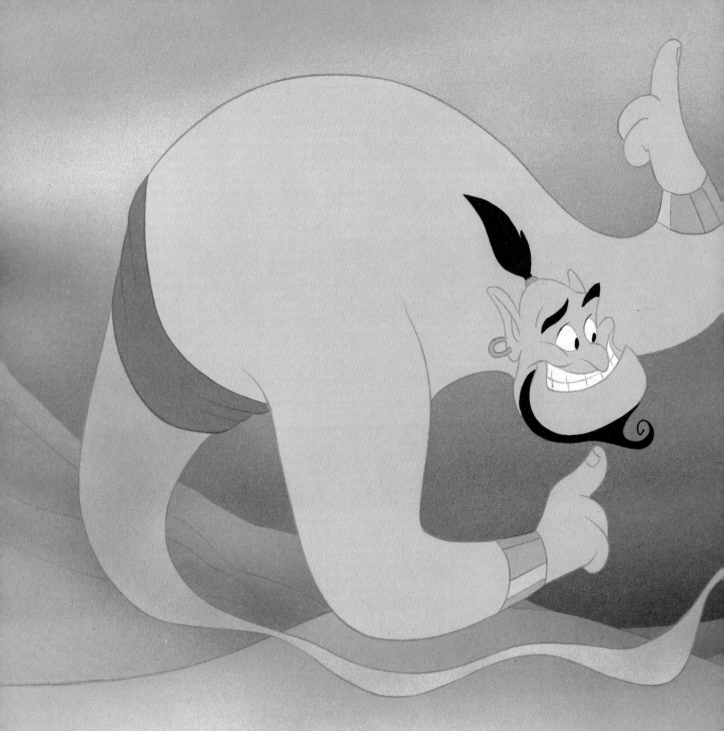

Aladdin dropped like a stone into the sea! As he sank below the waves, the lamp fell from his tunic. He strained against the ropes, until one hand was free. He rubbed the lamp.

The genie appeared. "Never fails!" he complained. "As soon as I get in the bathtub, somebody rubs the lamp! I guess you wish I'd get you out of this mess!"

Nearly unconscious, Aladdin nodded.

In the palace, Jasmine had made
a decision. "Father, I want to marry
Prince Ali!"

"Excellent!" the Sultan rejoiced.

Jafar stepped forward. "I'm
afraid that's impossible, Princess!
Prince Ali has . . . gone away!"

Jafar held his cobra staff before the Sultan's eyes. "But your father has something to tell you, Princess." Jafar smiled.

"You will . . . marry . . . Jafar!" the hypnotized Sultan droned.

"Never!" Jasmine cried. "Father! What's wrong with you?"

"I know!" said a voice from the doorway.

It was Aladdin. He snatched the cobra staff from Jafar and shattered it on the floor!

"This traitor has been hypnotizing you, your Majesty!" Aladdin said to the Sultan, who was now free of the spell.

Jafar ran from the room, but not before glimpsing the lamp in Aladdin's robe.

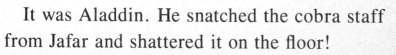

Later, hiding in his laboratory, Jafar plotted. "So Prince Ali is Aladdin!" he said. "And he has the lamp!"

At dawn the next morning, Iago crept into Aladdin's room and stole the lamp.

At last Jafar had the lamp! Eagerly, he
rubbed it.

The genie appeared.

"I am now your master!" Jafar bellowed.

"What a revolting development!" said the genie.

"I wish . . ." Jafar hesitated. "I wish to be
Sultan!"

That day, nearly everyone in the city of Agrabah was crowded beneath the palace balcony to hear the Sultan's happy news.

"My daughter has chosen Prince Ali to be her husband!" the Sultan announced. The crowd cheered.

Then the crowd gasped. The Sultan's royal robes vanished! Someone else appeared on the balcony wearing the Sultan's robes.

Jafar was now Sultan!

"We will never bow to you!" Aladdin said angrily.

Jafar held the magic lamp high. "Then you will cower!" he exclaimed, rubbing the lamp.

"Genie . . . I wish to be the most powerful sorcerer in the world!"

"I don't like it, but you got it, Master!" the genie replied.

"And for my first trick," the newly-made sorcerer said, "I banish Aladdin to the ends of the world!"

Bolts of lightning snapped from Jafar's fingertips, hurling Aladdin to the top of a palace tower. The tower snapped off and, like a rocket, it sped to the snowbound ends of the earth.

"How will I ever get out of here?" Aladdin groaned.

The answer to his question appeared from the toppled tower in the shape of Abu, followed by the magic carpet.

Meanwhile, back in Agrabah, the poor sultan was hanging from the ceiling of his throne room like a marionette, watching as Jafar ruled his kingdom.

"Bring me more wine, slave!" Jafar ordered Jasmine. Helpless in the sorcerer's power, she obeyed.

Clinging to the magic carpet, Aladdin and Abu swept out of the sky and into the palace!

"*You*!" Jafar snarled. "How many times do I have to get rid of you, boy?"

The sorcerer surrounded himself with a wall of flames.

"Are you afraid to fight me, you cowardly snake?" Aladdin challenged Jafar.

"A snake, am I?" Jafar replied. "So be it!"

Instantly Jafar turned himself into a huge cobra!
Aladdin and Jasmine drew back from the deadly
fangs.
"Did you think you could outwit the most
powerful sorcerer on earth?" hissed the cobra.

As the gigantic cobra raised its head to strike, Aladdin thought quickly.

"The genie has more power than you'll ever have, Jafar!" Aladdin exclaimed.

"You're right!" the power-mad Jafar agreed. He caught the lamp in his coils.

"Genie, my third wish is to be . . . a genie!"
The cobra vanished, and Jafar towered over
Aladdin in the shape of a genie. "Now I have
absolute power!" he crowed.

Then Jafar noticed what was happening. "What?" he shrieked. "I'm dissolving!"

In a moment, Jafar and Iago had disappeared forever imprisoned in a lamp that Aladdin was holding.

Then, with his third wish, Aladdin freed the genie.

"I'm going to miss you!" he said as the genie flew off to a new life.

The first thing the Sultan did when he became
Sultan again was to change the law. Princess
Jasmine could marry anyone she wished.

And since she wanted to marry Aladdin, that's
exactly what she did.